5/06

SALLY JEAN, the BICYCLE QUEEN

Cari Best

Pictures by
Christine Davenier

MELANIE KROUPA BOOKS
Farrar, Straus and Giroux • New York

For Peter and Greg and Alex and Seth
—C.B.
For Cecile Vignancour, the baby's queen!
—C.D.

Distributed in Canada by Douglas & McIntyre Ltd.
Color separations by Chroma Graphics PTE Ltd.
Printed and bound in the United States of America by Phoenix Color Corporation
Designed by Robbin Gourley
First edition, 2006
1 3 5 7 9 10 8 6 4 2

www.fsgkidsbooks.com

Library of Congress Cataloging-in-Publication Data
Best, Cari.
Sally Jean, the Bicycle Queen / Cari Best ; pictures by Christine Davenier.— 1st ed.
    p. cm.
Summary: When Sally Jean outgrows her beloved bicycle, Flash, she experiments with various ideas for acquiring a new, bigger one.
    ISBN-13: 978-0-374-36386-4
    ISBN-10: 0-374-36386-2
    [1. Bicycles and bicycling—Fiction.   2. Moneymaking projects—Fiction.
3. Self-reliance—Fiction.   4. Growth—Fiction.]   I. Davenier, Christine, ill.   II. Title.

PZ7.B46575Sal 2006
[E]—dc22

2004040461

When Sally Jean Sprockett was one year old, she sat in a seat on Mama's bike and watched the world go by: flowers and trees, pigeons and kites, helicopters and clouds—and the round of Mama's back.

"Hi!" she said to the big kids on their bikes.

When Sally Jean turned two, Granny got her a tricycle with streamers that swished and a horn that went "Onk! Onk!" She watched ants and spiders, caterpillars and bees, and two blue knees that pumped up and down.

"Hi!" she said to the big kids on their bikes.

Then she turned four, and Papa found her a yard-sale bike with two small wheels that hugged the ground. Sally Jean watched baby carriages and lawn mowers, squirrels and poodles, and pedals with reflectors that went round and round.

"Hi!" she said to the big kids on their bikes.

When she was five, the little wheels came off, and Mama held on while Sally Jean wobbled, then learned to pedal fast. Soon Mama let go and Sally Jean was off.

"Wait for meeee!" she called to the big kids on their bikes.

Sally Jean practiced going up the hill, and she practiced coming down. She zoomed across fields and boomed over bridges, cut sharp corners and skidded when she stopped. Her fingers knew their places on the handlebars and her feet fit the pedals like two snap-together blocks. Sally Jean and her bike became such good friends that she named it "Flash."

"I can't just call you 'Bike,'" she said, and then she sang:

I'm a plane, I'm a train,

I'm a girl up on a horse.

I'm Sally Jean, the Bicycle Queen,

And my bike is Flash, of course!

Then she was six, and Flash's seat needed raising. Mama showed her what to do with a push and a pull and a hit of her hammer.

"You're growing like a dandelion in spring," she said as Sally Jean watched. And soon Sally Jean was singing:

I can pop a wheelie, I can touch the sky,
I can pedal backwards, I can really fly!
I'm Sally Jean, the Bicycle Queen,
Just me, myself, and I!

When Sally Jean turned seven, the handlebars needed raising. Papa showed her what to do with a left and a right and a twist of his wrench. Sally Jean liked the way she and Flash got bigger together.

Sally Jean sang while she washed the wheels, and she sang while she shined the spokes.

Sally Jean was so busy singing that she never noticed how big she was growing.

By the time she turned eight, her knees bumped the handlebars and her shoes scraped the ground. She had to walk Flash up the hill for the very first time.

Sally Jean tried to raise Flash's seat. She tried to raise Flash's handlebars. But there was no more room for raising.

"What do I do now?" she asked.

"You can ride my bike when I'm at my trumpet lesson," said Stanley.

"You can sit while I pedal," said Andrew the Giant.

"You can pedal while I sit," said Murray.

"No thanks," Sally Jean said. "A Bicycle Queen needs to have her own bike."

Sally Jean tried skating places. But she always fell. She hopped and she skipped and she jumped and she ran. But nothing felt as good as riding.

"I just have to get another bike," she said.

"I wish I could help," said Papa, who needed new eyeglasses.
"Wait till next year," said Mama, who had to pay the dentist.
But Sally Jean couldn't wait. "What do I do now?" she asked.
Her neighbor, Mr. Mettle, had an idea.
"I could sure use your help in my yard," he said. "And I do have
lots of things you might like for your new bike."

So every day after school, Sally Jean helped Mr. Mettle organize his junk.

And when she was finished, she chose a basket, a light, and a can of sparkly paint.

But as she sat on the steps in front of her house and watched little kids and big kids and all kinds of bikes, Sally Jean wondered how she would ever get a bike of her own.

"What do I do now?" she asked.

"Fix my flat," said Murray.

"I can do that," said Sally Jean.

Then she thought about what else she could do.

The very next day, Sally Jean put up a sign:

PEDAL PUSHERS EVERYWHERE
HAVE FUN. LEARN TO FIX YOUR OWN BIKE
REASONABLE RATES. SEE SALLY JEAN, the B.Q.

And before long, she was in business.

But by the end of the summer, she'd
earned only enough money for two measly tires.

"What do I do now?" Sally Jean wondered.

She sat in a tree and looked all around and saw blue
jays and sparrows, woodpeckers and crows, and some
rusty old wheels she'd never noticed before. She saw buses
and trucks, motorcycles and cars, and some dusty old pedals
she couldn't ignore.

"This Bicycle Queen has an idea," she said, jumping down.

But Sally Jean's heart sank as she spun the floppy pedals and felt the dried-out tires. She sat there for a long time.

And then she started singing: "I Cycle, You Cycle, Recycle Junk!"

"That's my girl," said Mr. Mettle with a big smile.

Her friends didn't smile when they saw what she was carrying.
"That thing's ready for the dump," said Stanley.
"What a hunk of junk," said Andrew the Giant.
"It's all broken up," said Murray.

But Sally Jean said,

"Have no fear. The Bicycle Queen is here!"

At first everything looked hopeless.
But Sally Jean rolled up her sleeves
anyway and got to work.

And every afternoon after that,

she worked a little more . . .

and a little more . . .

and a little more . . .

until finally she had . . .

A BIKE!

LIGHTNING

Sally Jean even gave her new bike a name: "LIGHTNING."
"I can't just call you 'Bike,'" she said.

But something didn't feel right.

Until Sally Jean figured out what it was.
And fixed that, too.

I'm a plane, I'm a train,
I'm a boy up on a horse,
I'm Murray Bing, the Bicycle King . . .
And my bike is Flash, of course!

At last Sally Jean felt like singing again . . .

I can ride and whistle
I can fix a flat,

I can race a red bird,
I'm faster than a cat!

I'm Sally Jean, the Bicycle Queen. What do you think of that!